# The Little Book of

# BEDTIME STORIES

www.alligatorbooks.co.uk

The Alligator logo is a registered
trade mark of Alligator Books Ltd.

© 2012 Alligator Books Ltd

Published by Alligator Books Ltd
Gadd House, Arcadia Avenue
London N3 2JU
12060
Printed in India

# Contents

# The Nacho Monster

"I feel like a snack," Ronnie said to his friend Rick one morning. "Something crackly, crunchy, crisp and munchy."

"Cornflakes?" asked Rick.

"That's not what I want at all," said Ronnie. "I want a snack in a great big bag so you can munch as you go down the street."

Then Rick started hopping from one foot to the other. "I know! I know!" he yelled. "A MONSTER BAG OF NACHOS!"

"That's exactly what I want," agreed Ronnie. "Now let's go and get some!"

So off they raced to the nearest supermarket and went straight to the shelves that held the snacks.

They found fifty different flavoured crisps, cheesy puffs, onion hoops, loop-the-loops, even potato sticks that tasted of sardines.

BUT NO MONSTER BAGS OF NACHOS!!!

"We've run out!" said the manager.

"Run out?" gasped Ronnie and Rick together. "A supermarket with NO MONSTER BAGS OF NACHOS! That's unheard of!"

"My biggest customer has just bought the lot," said the manager.

"There he is going through the door."

"Who needs that many bags of nachos?" asked Ronnie.

"Let's find out," said Rick.

Once outside the supermarket, then boys stood still and stared.

"Tell me this isn't real," gulped Ronnie.

"Pinch me – I must be dreaming!" Rick's voice sounded ever so squeaky.

"HI THERE!" a loud voice boomed. Standing right in front of them was a Hairy Monster with a trolley full of MONSTER BAGS OF NACHOS!

"It's quite alright," the Hairy Monster assured them, "the manager lets me take the trolley home as long as I bring it back the next week."

"That's kind of him," squeakedRick.

"He must be able to trust you," blurted out Ronnie.

Then the Hairy Monster pointed his paw at the trolley full of nachos.

"We're having a party, do come and join us!"

Ronnie and Rick just nodded their heads, it's true to say they were lost for words.

"Hang on to my trolley!" the Hairy Monster boomed and took off like a rocket. "We'll go through the park, it's the quickest way back for me."

The three of them sped past the bandstand towards a clump of bushes.

"Help! Slow down!" both boys yelled and closed their eyes as they crashed through the bushes.

"Here we are," boomed the Hairy Monster. "Come and join the party!"

When Ronnie and Rick dared to open their eyes they were in the middle of a garden full of monsters of all shapes and sizes.

Balloons and streamers were everywhere, music was playing and there was lots of yummy, scrummy party food on the table.

"HERE COME THE MONSTER BAGS OF NACHOS!" boomed the Hairy Monster in a voice much louder than before, "AND I'VE BROUGHT ALONG TWO NEW FRIENDS!"

These monsters were a jolly lot… so Ronnie and Rick found. They loved to dance, play games and sing, but most of all… THEY LOVED EATING NACHOS!!!

And, as you know, so did Ronnie and Rick.

When all the nachos had gone and the party came to an end, Ronnie and Rick thought it was time for them to go too.

"Shall we take your trolley back to the supermarket for you?" the boys asked the Hairy Monster.

"No need!" he boomed "I'll be going there as usual next week to buy all the MONSTER BAGS OF NACHOS."

"Save some for us!" laughed Ronnie and Rick. Then they closed their eyes, and when they opened them, they were back in the park next to the bandstand.

If your supermarket runs out of MONSTER BAGS OF NACHOS every week...I'm sure you can guess were they've gone!

# Whitney the Witch

When Charlie went back to school one Monday morning he could hardly believe his eyes. Sitting at the desk next to him was a little girl dressed as a witch.

"Please take care of our new pupil," the teacher, Miss Plum, said to Charlie.

"Her name is Whitney and she will be with us for the rest of the year."

"Do you always come to school dressed in that weird outfit?" asked Charlie the moment Miss Plum turned her back.

Whitney shrugged her shoulders and looked puzzled, "Every witch I know dresses like this."

"I don't believe it," Charlie sighed, "I have to look after a girl who thinks she's a real witch. Great!"

Charlie slumped down in his chair and put his head on the desk with a mighty thump.

"Ouch! That hurt!" howled Charlie as a big purple bruise appeared on his brow.

"This will make it better," said Whitney with a sweet smile. She tapped Charlie's head with her wand and the bruise vanished.

Right there and then Charlie knew she was a real witch, and that a real witch with a real magic wand could make school very interesting.

"Do I call you Witch Whitney?" asked Charlie.

"Just Whitney will do," the young witch replied unpacking her school bag.

As the weeks went by Charlie discovered Whitney was the
cleverest of witches. She got top marks in every test, and her
homework was always correct.

"Why do you bother doing any work at all?" Charlie asked
Whitney one day. "Just wave your wand and your lessons
will be done."

"That's strictly against the rules!" Whitney sounded quite
shocked. "Witches must learn things for themselves and never use
their magic at school."

"You made the bruise on my head disappear by magic," Charlie pointed out to her.

"That was an emergency," whispered Whitney.

Then one morning Whitney went into Miss Plum's office to have her books marked, and she left her magic wand on the desk.

Without thinking what might happen, Charlie grabbed the wand and pointed it at a computer, "Vanish!" he ordered... AND IT DID!

Not satisfied with that, he pointed the wand at a model of a dinosaur on Miss Plum's desk, "Come alive!" he ordered... AND IT DID!

As the dinosaur lumbered through the classroom it kept growing and growing. By the time it had crossed the hall and stepped outside into the playground...IT WAS ENORMOUS!!!

The bell for the morning break had just rung and the children had gone out to play.

"What is that?" shouted the big boys when they spotted the dinosaur.

"Is it going to eat me?" asked one of the little girls.

"He's a dinosaur, and he won't eat you because he's a vegetarian," said Whitney, who had just come out into the playground followed by Charlie.

"That's alright then!" yelled the children. "Come on, let's play with the dinosaur!"

Charlie looked sheepishly at Whitney. "Sorry for using your magic wand. Mind if I go and play with the dinosaur?"

To his amazement Whitney wasn't in the least bit cross. "I've broken the first rule of magic," she said. "You must always keep your wand with you at all times, so it's really my fault."

Then she started to giggle, "I'm going to play with the dinosaur too!"

No one seemed to mind a dinosaur at school. Miss Plum took to him right away because he wiped his feet well on wet days, and kept the children quiet with his wonderful stories.

The dinosaur delighted
the ladies who served the
school lunch, he always
ate up his greens, and so
thechildren did too!

At the end of each day,
when it was time to go
home, Miss Plum had a
golden rule, "The dinosaur
must be back on my desk
as soon as the home
bell rings!"

Then Whitney would wave her magic wand and the dinosaur
became a model once more.

# Red the Rescuer

Big Joe and his mighty tow truck, Red, were always prepared for sudden emergencies. They would travel anywhere, any time, answering calls for help however difficult or dangerous.

Red and Big Joe's work began very early one morning. The bridge across the harbour was stuck fast, it had to be released before ships could pass through once more.

So Big Joe hooked up the crane, Red gave one powerful tug, and the bridge was open!

"Try and get that bridge mended today!" called Big Joe as they drove away.

Next came a major situation. A volcano, far beyond the mountains, was about to blow!

Taking great care, Red pushed a giant boulder over a cliff. Down the valley it hurtled, flew up and landed right on top of the volcano!

Well done, Red! You've saved the valley!

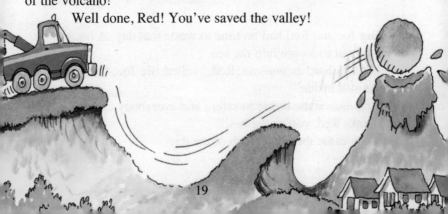

Big Joe and Red had no time to waste that day. A house was about to topple into the sea.

"Pull as hard as you can, Red," yelled Big Joe, "there are folks still inside!"

Red moved the house to safety and everybody cheered, "Thanks Red, you're the best!"

Then came the biggest job of the day.

"The Space Centre's transporter has broken down," said Big Joe, "and the launch is in less than one hour."

With his super strength, Red managed to drag the transporter and the Space Shuttle to the launch on time.

Countdown began…and in ten seconds Red watched with Big Joe as the Space Shuttle blasted off into space…

we have lift off!!!

But was that their biggest job today? Perhaps not!

A great herd of elephants had to be moved across an enormous park.

"I'm sure Red can do it," said Big Joe, "if they all promise to stand still and don't run away!"

Then on the way home Red began to cough and splutter. Big Joe quickly switched off the engine.

"I'll find out what's the matter," said Big Joe, and he jumped down from the cab, climbed on top of the wheel and opened Red's bonnet...there was a loud hissing sound and a cloud of white steam.

"A water hose is leaking." Big Joe sounded worried. "I'm sorry, Red, I haven't got a spare." Big Joe and Red had been busy helping people all day, let's hope someone will help them now.

As Big Joe sat by the side of the road wondering what to do, a little boy rode up on his bicycle.

"What's the matter with Red?" he asked Big Joe.

"Leaking water hose," replied Big Joe.

"No problem," smiled the boy, and he reached into his pocket. "You can have my repair kit, I use it to mend my bike tyres."

"You're a boy in a million!" laughed Big Joe. "You can tell all your friends that today you rescued Red the Rescuer!"

# Lilith's Fairy Dust Hat

Lilith, the littlest fairy, had lost her flower petal hat.

"I need a brand new one," she said, and flew off to look for a new one right away.

The littlest fairy picked the first flower she came to and popped it on top of her head.

"How do I look?" she asked a dragonfly that was hovering close by.

"As silly as can be!" he replied.

"Then how about a red poppy hat?" Lilith asked him when she had chosen another flower.

"Poppies make you sneeze, and by the way, you have a smudge of black pollen right on the end of your nose!" and he fluttered back to his home by the river tittering all the way.

Next Lilith tried a daisy hat, but it was far too heavy and a wee bit old-fashioned.

"I know!" cried the littlest fairy.
"A foxglove bell would fit me just beautifully!"

But she was wrong. The hat was so big, Lilith was lost inside and had to call for help.

Now the Fairy Queen (who always knew what was happening to every fairy), was absolutely brilliant at choosing hats.

"For you, the softest thistledown," said the Fairy Queen, and with a wave of her magic wand, and a sprinkling of fairy dust... there was Lilith's new hat!

How it sparkled and twinkled, how it glittered in the sunlight.

"A perfect hat for my littlest fairy," said the Fairy Queen smiling at Lilith.

# Grandad's Birthday Present

It was Grandad's birthday tomorrow and Archie's mum and dad were trying to think of a present.

"Chocolates would be nice," suggested Mum.

"We buy those every year," Archie sighed.

"How about a book on gardening?" asked Dad.

"Boring, boring, boring," groaned Archie.

"Then you think of something," said Mum and Dad together.

"A robot!" said Archie firmly. "Grandad would just love a robot!"

So off they droved to a huge toy store on the edge of town and bought a robot.

Archie took great care of it on the way home, and then gave Grandad the robot on his birthday morning.

"I've always wanted one of those robots," chuckled Grandad. "He can help me make things in my workshop!"

"Pardon?" said Mum frowning.

"What did he say?" said Dad.

"I just knew he'd love it," grinned Archie.

And after Grandad had eaten three slices of birthday cake and read all his cards, he led the robot into his workshop and closed the door.

"Leave Grandad alone with his present," his mum told Archie. "You can come into the kitchen and help me with lunch."

As Archie peeled potatoes and chopped up carrots, he could hear the oddest sounds coming from his Grandad's workshop…hammering, tapping, clinking and clunking, and a noise that sounded like wings flapping or beaks snapping.

Archie could stand it no longer. He rushed out of the kitchen and thumped on the workshop door.

"Come in, Archie, and see what we've made," Grandad called from inside.

And when Archie opened the door…this is what he found!

Grandad and the robot had been very busy indeed.

"I knew you'd like the robot," Archie gasped as he stared around.

"It's the best!" grinned Grandad.

32

# Jessie's Little Foal

When her pony, Candy, had a foal, it took Jessie ages to choose a name.

"She's so special," said Jessie when she looked into the stable the day the little foal was born. "I need to think of a really special name."

"How about Dasher, or Dancer or Prancer?" suggested her brother, just teasing.

"They're the names of Santa's reindeer," said Jessie, "so stop being silly!"

"You wouldn't let me choose the name anyway," shouted her brother, and he ran off leaving Jessie gazing fondly at the foal.

A whole week passed and still Jessie hadn't come up with a name, it was so difficult.

"Come along, sweetheart," Jessie said to the foal as she opened the stable door – that was the name she was using – just for the time being.

The little foal followed Jessie everywhere. When she was busy in the stable yard, the foal stayed close behind her. Sometimes she got in the way and jobs had to be done again, but Jessie didn't mind at all.

"You were only trying to help, sweetheart," smiled Jessie giving the foal a hug.

"I see you've still got your shadow with you!" her brother called to her from across the yard.

"SHADOW!" cried Jessie jumping up and down with delight. "Shadow is brilliant, I can't think of a better name!"

So, thanks to her brother, from then on the little foal was called Shadow, and on a day in summer she lived up to her name!

One weekend, a horse show was being held in a field near Jessie's home. She was taking along her pony, Candy, to compete in some of the events.

On the morning of the show Jessie got up earlier than usual. She needed plenty of time to groom her pony so she would look her very best.

Jessie fetched her brushes and began by cleaning Candy's coat, next she combed her mane and long flowing tail.

"Nearly done!" she said to Candy, and last of all, she oiled her pony's hooves and gave her coat a final polish with a sheepskin mitt.

"Now it's my turn to get ready," said Jessie, and she hurried into the house.

All this time Shadow had been trying to poke her head over
the stable door, and when Jessie returned dressed up for the
show, she couldn't resist going into the stable to give the foal
a great big hug.

"Wish us luck, Shadow!" laughed Jessie. Then she saddled up
Candy, rode out of the yard and galloped off to the horse show.

Before too long, Shadow began to miss Jessie and Candy
and was anxious to see where they had gone. To her surprise
when she tried to poke her head over the stable door... it swung
wide open!

Jessie was in a hurry and couldn't have closed it properly.

Out trotted the curious little foal, across the yard, past the rest of the stables and into the garden.

Now Shadow had never been in a garden before, and couldn't work out what it was for. So she rolled up and down the lawn and raced in and out of the flowerbeds.

Still looking for Jessie and Candy, Shadow managed to squeeze through the hedge, and then she set off down the lane towards the horse show.

Once through the main gate, she could see Jessie and Candy in the show ring, and a judge was presenting Jessie with a large silver cup.

A crowd was standing watching, and when they spotted Shadow entering the ring they all started to clap. The little foal thought this was great fun, so she tossed her head and bowed, and then trotted across the grass daintily.

As she reached Jessie and Candy, a voice over a loudspeaker announced, "This is the winner of the Prettiest Foal in the Show Competition!"

"That's you, Shadow! You've won first prize!" exclaimed Jessie taking hold of her foal's head collar.

When the show ended, Jessie led Candy and Shadow back home.

"This explains why you are covered in flowers," said Jessie as they walked passed the ruined flowerbeds.

But how could Jessie be cross with Shadow for following her and Candy to the show? None of this would have happened if Jessie had closed the stable door properly!

And Shadow did win first prize for the Prettiest Foal in the Show - so it all turned out quite well after all!

# Pete and Branco, Range Riders

Pete lived on The Three Horseshoe Ranch and rode a horse called Branco.

Every year the town nearby held a rodeo and Pete went along to watch the contests in the ring. Folks came from near and far to see the cowboys test their skills. The rodeo show was always exciting and often very dangerous.

To begin with, there was bareback riding on broncos that bucked and reared. Some of the more daring cowboys tried riding bulls, and others jumped from their horses and wrestled steers to the ground.

When the time came for cattleroping, Pete always pushed his way to the front of the ring, and climbed up on top of the fence to get a better view.

Pete had just been given his own lasso, he could do a few rope tricks, but nothing like the rodeo cowboys.

"I need lots of practise if I'm going to be a real cowboy," thought Pete as he headed back to the ranch, "then I'll be a rodeo star some day."

And how hard Pete practised! Every day he stood outside with his lasso, spinning the rope into small loops, large loops – even figures of eight.

"Time to try roping," said Pete out loud, and he tossed his lasso over the nearest fence post. "Right on target!" shouted Pete, very pleased with himself. So he tried once more... and did it again!

By the end of that morning he'd lassoed every fence post in the yard, and never missed one!

From then on, Pete lassoed everything in sight. One day he lassoed his grandma snoozing on the porch in the sun.

"Time to try roping on the move!" Pete declared, and he saddled up Branco and rode away.

Beyond The Three Horseshoe Ranch grew lots of giant cactus…just perfect for Pete to lasso.

"I'll never do it!" yelled Pete as Branco galloped past the first one at top speed… but he roped the cactus easily.

Sometimes Branco would swerve, just to make it harder, but Pete lassoed a giant cactus every single time.

"Time to rope my first steer," said Pete patting his horse's neck. Branco tossed his head and snorted loudly… was this really a good idea?

Pete stood up in his stirrups and gazed across the ranch. A herd of cattle were grazing in the distance but they were too far away.

"We'll have to wait and rope my first steer tomorrow," Pete told Branco, and he pulled on the reins and headed for home.

On his way back to The Three Horseshoe Ranch, Pete and Branco had to cross a railway line. As they neared the track Pete was certain he could hear snorting and bellowing.

There, standing in the middle of the line, was a very angry looking bull. "He's a long way from the herd," said Pete with dismay. "We're going to have to take him back."

When the bull spotted Pete and Branco, he stopped bellowing and at once began to paw the ground.

Suddenly a whistle blew!

"There's a train coming and the bull is in the way!" yelled Pete.

45

"Come on, Branco, it's up to us!"

The whistle blew again and kept on blowing. This meant the driver had seen them and was trying to stop the train.

Would he make it in time?

Pete grabbed the lasso, swung it round twice then tossed it over the animal's head.

He's roped the bull! Hurrah!

Slowly and carefully Branco trotted away, pulling the bull behind him on the rope.

SCREEEECH!

The train came to a halt just as the line was cleared.

Down jumped the driver looking very relieved. "You and your horse have saved my train and all the passengers. When we reach town the Sheriff will hear how brave you have been!"

Before they went home Pete and Branco led the bull back to the herd. And when they rode through the gates of The Three Horseshoe Ranch, the Sheriff was waiting to thank them.

"One day, you'll be champion of our town rodeo," he laughed shaking Pete's hand, "and I'm sure you'll be riding Branco!"

# Musical Party Dresses

Rosie, Gem, Tilda and Bridget dressed alike at school, they always wore their school uniforms, because that was the rule. But when they went to parties they liked to look different!

One afternoon when the girls arrived home from school, their mum had something exciting to tell them.

"You've been invited to a party," said Mum. "It's at five o'clock tomorrow, and you have to dress up." The four girls shrieked. "We don't have any dressing up clothes to wear!" they cried, "and tomorrow is a school day!"

"No problem," said Mum. "I can go to the shops in the morning and choose some great outfits for you."

Rosie, Gem, Tilda and Bridget ran to their mum and gave her a hug, then they all stepped back and took a deep breath.

"I want to go as a princess," said Rosie.

"I want to go as a ballerina," said Gem.

"I want to go as a mermaid," said Tilda.

"And I want to go in a sparkly dress," giggled Bridget.

Next morning Mum went off to the shops, and much later came back with loads of parcels.

The four girls talked about the party all day at school, and came home feeling very excited.

When Mum unpacked the dresses, Rosie, Gem, Tilda and Bridget were thrilled to bits.

"I don't know which one to choose," said Rosie.

"Nor do we," said Tilda and Gem.

"They're all so sparkly," giggled Bridget.

The four girls couldn't decide what to wear, and they changed their minds several times.

Mum, however, knew exactly how to solve the problem. She put the dresses into a large bag and switched on some music.

"Pass the bag round, girls!" she shouted. "When the music stops, the one holding the bag puts her hand inside and pulls out a dress for the party."

The first time the music stopped, Rosie was holding the bag. "Great!" she cried. "Mine's the mermaid costume!" and she passed the bag on.

When the music stopped again, it was Tilda this time. "Brilliant!" she laughed, "I've got the ballerina's dress!" and she passed the bag on.

Gem was next when the music stopped. "Wow!" she gasped. "I'm going dressed as a princess!" and she passed the bag on to Bridget. Hers was the last dress of all, and when she put her hand in the bag, she pulled out the final costume.

"Mine is the sparkliest one of all!" she giggled.

The bag was empty, and Rosie, Gem, Tilda and Bridget were ready to go to the party.

# An Invitation to a Party

Fairy Thistledown and her sister Angelica
had slept rather late this particular morning.
Outside the sun was shining brightly, the
birds were singing, and most of the fairy
folk who lived nearby had been up and
about since daybreak.

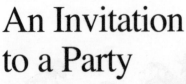

A velvet-coated bumble-bee with a satchel by his side had been
tapping on Thistledown and Angelica's front door for ages. He was
just about to go away when he noticed that the fairies' bedroom
window was wide open, so up he flew. The sound of his noisy
buzzing awoke the two sleeping fairies, and they looked out of the
window in surprise.

"Don't hold me up, I'm in a hurry!"
the bumblebee buzzed
crossly. "Special delivery, sign here,
please!" He thrust a letter through
the open window and off he sped.

"It looks like an invitation,"
yawned Angelica still drowsy.

The letter was written on a
rose petal tied with a cobweb
covered in dewdrop pearls.

"It's from the Fairy Queen,"
gasped Thistledown, who by
now was wideawake. "We've
both been invited to a party at
the palace…and it's today!"

Angelica, still in her fairy
nightclothes, fluttered round the
bedroom shrieking, "We haven't
got a thing to wear!"

"Of course we have," said Thistledown calmly. "Our wardrobe is full of party dresses." She was a bit older than Angelica and could always solve any problem.

"I'll never be able to choose one in time for the party," wailed Angelica still fluttering round.

"Then let me choose for you," said Thistledown trying to be helpful. "I suggest your white organdie one trimmed with gold lace."

"Of course!" cried Angelica, "I'll wear my satin slippers with the green ribbons."

"Perfect!" agreed Thistledown. "I'll go in lavender and palest pink speckled with sparkling beads."

"That sounds perfect too," laughed Angelica and she rushed over to the wardrobe to find their dresses.

There is so much to do when you are going to a party – bracelets to find, necklaces to try on, and what about your hair?

It took the two fairies all morning to get ready…they even forgot to have lunch.

Every time Thistledown and Angelica went to a party, the butterflies in the garden pulled their fairy carriage made of plaited ribbons covered with flowers.

"I'll find out if the butterflies are ready!" called Thistledown as she went outside.

"And I'll check what time we should arrive at the Fairy Queen's palace," said Angelica reading their invitation.

Suddenly Thistledown heard a tiny scream and Angelica came
flying out into the garden. "Our invitation is for this evening,
and not this afternoon," and the shocked fairy read out loud,
"You are both invited to the Fairy Queen's Dusk till Dawn Party
at the Palace."

At once both fairies realised that the butterflies couldn't possibly
pull their carriage at night, for they folded their wings as soon as the
sun set, then slept all night until dawn.

Poor Angelica started to cry, she felt so disappointed. Thankfully
Thistledown knew how to solve the problem, and flew off to talk to
the butterflies.

When she came back she was smiling. "Don't be sad," she told Angelica. "Everything is arranged, we can go to the party tonight."

While Angelica dried her eyes, Thistledown popped inside the house and made her sister some of her favourite elderflower waffles, just to cheer her up.

And that evening, when it was dusk and the first stars began to twinkle in the sky, their carriage arrived at the door pulled by silver-winged moths…who were the butterflies' cousins!

They even brought a few fireflies along to light Thistledown and Angelica's way to the palace. Problem solved!

# The Pirate Twins

Ollie and Matt were identical twins. They looked alike of course, but they never dressed the same…except when they were playing pirates. Then it was impossible to tell one from the other.

One day Great-gran came for a visit. "Call yourselves pirates, boys?" and she tittered. "Real pirates always wear eye patches!" and she pulled a couple out of her handbag.

"Brilliant!" cried Ollie.

"Cool!" cried Matt.

"Be prepared, both of you," smiled Great-gran, "strange and exciting things will happen when you wear them," and she settled down in an armchair for a nap.

The instant Ollie and Matt put on the eye patches, they whizzed high in the air surrounded by showers of sparks and a cloud of blue smoke. Round and round they whirled, then plunged downwards and landed with a thump.

"Where on earth are we?" gasped Ollie.

"On the deck of a ship," replied Matt quietly, "and it's a pirate ship!"

"That's impossible!" said Ollie trying to keep his balance as the ship moved with the waves.

All that Matt could do was stare. "Look at those cannons, and this ship is flying the Jolly Roger!!!"

"There's no land in sight," called Ollie running to the ship's rail and gazing out to sea.

But his twin brother didn't reply, for a powerful hand had grabbed him by the shoulder.

"Stowaway aboard, captain!" yelled an evil-looking man as he dragged Matt across the deck.

Ollie quickly hid behind a barrel trying to think what to do next.

When Matt looked up, standing before him was the most fearsome man he had ever seen. He was the terror of the high seas…Captain Blackheart.

"Stowaway, eh?" he growled. "He's come to steal our treasure more likely. Rope him to the mast where I can keep my good eye on him!"

While the pirates were tying up his twin brother, Ollie crept across the deck and climbed up the rigging – that way he could see what was happening.

As Matt struggled to get free, he noticed that the deck of the ship was littered with doubloons and pieces of eight that had spilled out of a large chest.

"He's seen pirate gold, boys!" shouted Captain Blackheart, "and you all know the punishment for that!"

"Make him walk the plank!" yelled the crew angrily.

Was that really going to happen to poor Matt?

Time for some quick thinking by Ollie. He decided to play a trick on the pirates...identical twins play this kind of trick on people all the time!

As Matt set foot on the plank, Ollie shouted down from the rigging, "This ship is doomed if you make me walk the plank!"

This made Captain Blackheart and his crew shake with fear as they stared up at Ollie.

"That boy is bewitched!" screamed one of the pirates. "He can fly!"

Matt, meanwhile, had jumped down from the plank and was standing in the middle of the deck.

When the pirates noticed him, their faces went pale with fright. "If any harm should befall me," Matt spoke in his scariest voice, "you and your ship will roam the high seas for all time."

Just at the right moment, Ollie jumped down from the rigging and stood next to his twin, Matt. Seeing them together was too much for the pirates, and they fled in all directions.

"We tricked them, didn't we, Matt?" laughed Ollie. "And I think I've figured out the way to get home. Great-gran's eye patches brought us here, they'll take us back again!"

So Ollie and Matt pulled off their eye patches immediately, and in a shower of sparks and a cloud of blue smoke, they whizzed through the air and landed with a thump right next to Great-gran's armchair.

"Met Captain Blackheart and his pirate crew, then?" asked Great-gran giving the boys a knowing wink.

"We sure did!" Ollie and Matt replied, and both of them pulled a golden doubloon from their pockets and handed them to Great-gran.